World of Reading

MARVEL
SPIDER-MAN
LEVEL
2
+ FUN SCIENCE FACTS

Down to a Science!

Adapted by **Alexandra West**

Based on the animated series Marvel's Spider-Man

MARVEL

Los Angeles
New York

MARVEL
marvelkids.com

SUSTAINABLE
FORESTRY
INITIATIVE
Certified Sourcing
www.sfiprogram.org
SFI-01415

Printed in the United States of America
First Edition, September 2017 10 9 8 7 6 5 4 3 2 1
Library of Congress Control Number: 2017906489
FAC-029261-17223
ISBN 978-1-368-00859-4

Spider-Man is a Super Hero.
He has a proto-suit.
He has web-shooters.
Spider-Man protects the city.

Suddenly, Spider-Man is attacked by Vulture! Vulture is a Super Villain. He uses his sonic scream.

A sonic boom is created when an object travels faster than the speed of sound.

Spider-Man has an idea.
He puts webbing over his ears.
Spider-Man is ready to
defeat Vulture!

Spider-Man's web-shooters break!
"How about a little gravity?"
Spider-Man says.
He webs a streetlight and grabs
Vulture's leg.

Gravity is a force that tries to pull objects to each other.

Spider-Man throws Vulture.
Vulture crashes into a truck.
“Nice try!” Vulture says.
He uses his sonic scream.

BUGLE

Glass falls from the buildings.
The officers are in danger!
Spider-Man must save the officers.

All objects free-fall at
the same rate of speed.

Spider-Man creates a web ball
to protect the officers.
“Thanks, web head!” the officer says.
“It’s Spider-Man,” Spider-Man says,
“and I’m late for school!”

Spider-Man is really Peter Parker.
Peter is a high school student.
Peter loves science.

Science is the study of the world through observation and experimentation.

Harry Osborn is Peter's friend.
Harry tells Peter about Horizon High.
Horizon High is a science school.

Peter Parker goes to school.
He listens to Max Modell speak.
Max is the dean of Horizon High.

Max presents an equation.
If Peter can solve the equation,
then he can go to Horizon High.

Did you know that
111,111,111 × 111,111,111 = 12,345,678,987,654,321?

Harry, Anya, and Miles
are students at Horizon High.
They are very smart.
They make robots and
powerful machines.

More than a million industrial robots are in use today.

Peter's spider-sense tingles.
Something is not right.

Anya presents her project.
The machine uses a rare metal.
It creates energy.

Lasers cannot be seen in space because they have no matter.

Anya turns it on.
The machine
crashes!
It fires dangerous
laser beams.

Peter puts on his proto-suit.
Peter becomes Spider-Man!
Spider-Man swings into action.

The tensile strength of spider silk is very similar to that of steel.

Spider-Man swings toward the stage.
He dodges the lasers.

Spider-Man swings onto the stage.
Spider-Man stops the machine.
It lets out one final explosion.

EXIT

The explosion sets the room on fire! It also burns Spider-Man's proto-suit. "Luckily, I have my Parker clothes," Spider-Man says.

A single candle flame can typically burn at around 1,800°F.

Spider-Man puts on his Parker clothes.
Peter needs to put out the fire—fast!
He sees Max's equation.
It gives him an idea.

Water has three different states:
liquid, solid, and gas.

He reworks the machine.
It pulls water from the air.
It creates a rain cloud that
puts out the fire.

Peter saves the school.
But Anya is mad.
Her machine is broken.
“My hard work is ruined!” Anya says.

When an electric machine gets wet, the water can cause it to “short-circuit.”

Max is impressed.
Peter solved his equation and saved everyone.
Max offers Peter a spot at Horizon High.
"I accept!" Peter says.

Why did the machine crash?
Peter's teacher blames Harry!
He has a photo on his cell phone.
Harry is suspended from Horizon High

Cell phones communicate to each other through radio waves.

Suddenly, Vulture attacks!
He uses his sonic scream.

Vulture takes the rare metal
from Anya’s machine.
“Exactly what I have been
looking for,” Vulture says.

Peter puts on his proto-suit.
"You're not getting away
this time!" Spider-Man says.

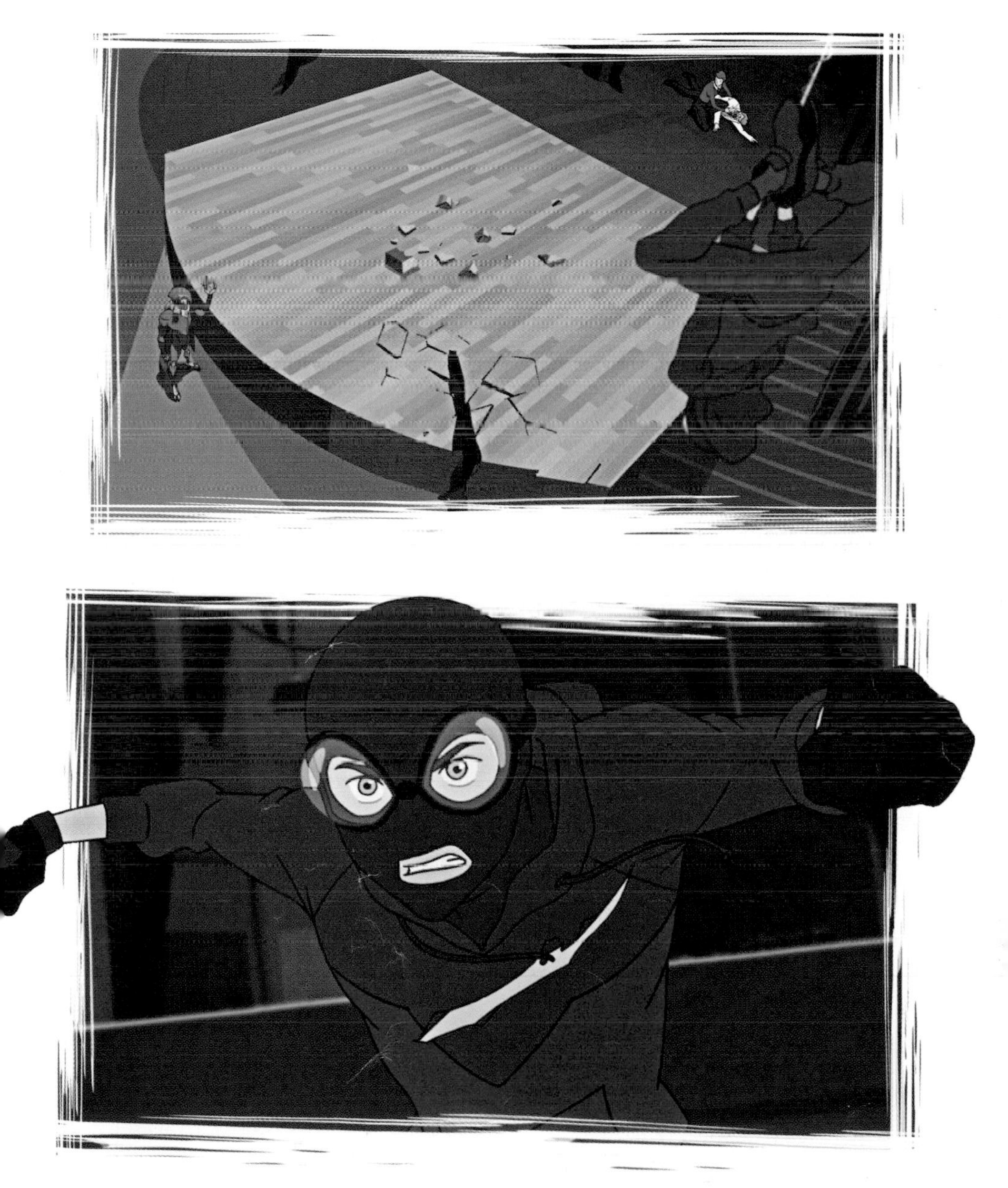

THWIP!

Spider-Man webs Vulture's mask.

CRACK!

Spider-Man hits Vulture hard.

The Vulture is defeated!

The Darwin's bark spider in Madagascar makes the world's largest webs.

The officers arrest Vulture.
"Thanks, Spider-Man!"
the officer says.
"You finally got my name right!"
Spider-Man says.

Peter saves the day.
It is time for school.
Peter goes to Horizon High.
It's going to be an interesting
school year.